MANHATTAN

for Millie

MANHATTAN

a story by Jean Christian Knaff

faber and faber

LONDON · BOSTON

Manhattan was very small. He lived in a country of empty castles and quiet volcanoes. He had only his tiny horse for company.

Often Manhattan was unhappy.
Sometimes his head hurt,

but not for long.

Sometimes he felt tired,

and he would sleep for a while.

But mostly he was lonely.
He longed for someone to talk to.

Then one day, at the foot of the Blue Volcano,

he met Julia.
They talked and talked.

Julia told him of places he had never seen. Manhattan had an idea. He would show Julia his country.

Together they went to the Big Black Door,

and through to the stairs behind.

They climbed and climbed
to the top!

Outside the night was clear and bright, and they could see for miles and miles.
The moon was so close they could have touched it.

Julia smiled.
She would stay.

First published in 1987
by Faber and Faber Limited
3 Queen Square, London WC1N 3AU

Printed in Great Britain by
Jolly & Barber Ltd, Rugby, Warwickshire

British Library Cataloguing in Publication Data

Knaff, Jean Christian
Manhattan.
I. Title
813'.54 [J]   PZ7
ISBN 0-571-14653-8